D0465551

Dora's Picnic

by Christine Ricci
illustrated by Susan Hall

SCHOLASTIC INC.
New York Toronto London Auckland Sydney
Mexico City New Delhi Hong Kong Buenos Aires

Based on the TV series *Dora the Explorer*® as seen on Nick Jr.®

ISBN 0-439-53977-3

12 11 10 9 8 7 6 5 4 3 2 1   3 4 5 6 7 8/0

Printed in the U.S.A.

First Scholastic printing, September 2003

Hi! I am . We are
going to a picnic at Play
Park! Play Park has a 🛝,
SLIDE

a 🟫, and 🛝.
SANDBOX   SWINGS

My **mami** is helping me make -and-

PEANUT-BUTTER   JELLY

sandwiches for the picnic.

 is my best friend.

BOOTS

He loves 🍌!

BANANAS

 BOOTS **has a bunch of** 🍌 **BANANAS**
for the picnic.

BENNY is riding his **BICYCLE** to the picnic.

He is carrying juice

APPLE

in his 🧺.

BASKET

Here comes the .

BIG RED CHICKEN

The has a big of

BIG RED CHICKEN   BAG

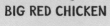 for the picnic.

POPCORN

Yummy!

Look!  has a bowl of

BABY BLUE BIRD

fruit in her .

WAGON

The fruit bowl has ,

BANANAS

, and .

APPLES   **GRAPES**

What did  bring to the picnic?

TICO

 TICO **brought** . **BREAD**

The **is filled with** **BREAD**

BLUEBERRIES **and** **!** **NUTS**

made to share with everyone.

ISA

CUPCAKES

I like chocolate  CUPCAKES with PINK icing. What kind do you like?

Look out for  .
SWIPER
He will try to swipe
the food we brought.

 is hiding behind

SWIPER

the 🌳.

TREE

Say, "Swiper, no swiping!"

Yay! You stopped 🦊!

SWIPER

We made it to Play Park!
This  is perfect for
TABLE
our picnic. But first we
want to play!

likes to go down

TICO

the **.**

SLIDE

BABY BLUE BIRD is making a **SAND CASTLE**

in the **SANDBOX**.

The pushes
BIG RED CHICKEN   BOOTS

and on the .
ISA   SWINGS

This is the best picnic!
We can all share the food.
What would **you** bring
to a picnic?